100 FACTS
Whales & Dolphins

100 FACTS
Whales & Dolphins

Steve Parker

Miles Kelly

First published in 2006 by Miles Kelly Publishing Ltd
Harding's Barn, Bardfield End Green, Thaxted, Essex, CM6 3PX

Copyright © Miles Kelly Publishing Ltd 2006

This edition updated 2014, printed 2022

8 10 12 14 15 13 11 9 7

Publishing Director Belinda Gallagher
Creative Director Jo Cowan
Editors Amanda Askew, Claire Philip
Volume Designers Elaine Wilkinson, Venita Kidwai, Rob Hale
Image Manager Liberty Newton
Indexer Marie Lorimer
Production Jennifer Brunwin
Reprographics Stephan Davis
Assets Lorraine King

All rights reserved. No part of this publication may be reproduced, stored in
a retrieval system, or transmitted by any means, electronic, mechanical, photocopying,
recording or otherwise, without the prior permission of the copyright holder.

ISBN 978-1-78989-404-2

Printed in China

British Library Cataloguing-in-Publication Data
A catalogue record for this book is available from the British Library

ACKNOWLEDGEMENTS

The publishers would like to thank Stuart Jackson-Carter for the artwork he contributed to this book.
All other artwork from the Miles Kelly Artwork Bank

The publishers would like to thank the following sources for the use of their photographs:
t = top, b = bottom, l = left, r = right, c = centre, bg = background
Cover (front) Stuart Westmorland/Corbis Documentary/Getty
Ardea.com 30 M.Watson **FLPA.com** 23(t) Flip Nicklin/Minden Pictures; 34 Hiroya Minakuchi/Minden Pictures;
41 Tui De Roy/Minden Pictures **Fotolia.com** 9 Alexey Khromushin **iStockphoto.com** 9(c) Håkan Karlsson
Getty 31(b) Stephen Frink; **Naturepl.com** 21(t) Jeff Rotman; 26 Tony Wu; 32(m) Mark Carwardine; 36–37 Tony
Wu; 38–39 Mark Carwardine; 46 Bryan and Cherry Alexander **Oceanwidelmages.com** 33
Photoshot 27(b) Woodfall **Rex Features** 45(tr) Moviestore Collection/Rex Features **SeaPics** 8 Christopher Swann;
16-17 **Science Photo Library** 20–21 Christopher Swann **Topfoto** 40(b) Fine Art Images/HIP; 47 David Fleetham
ShutterstockPremier 2–3 Nolte Lourens; 5 Anders Peter Photography; 9(b) Willyam Bradberry; 10 Shane Gross,
(b) Shannon Workman; 13–14 Menna; 13 Jan-Dirk Hansen; 15(t) Johan_R, (c) Teo Dominguez; 15(b) Steve
Noakes; 17 Ivan Cholakov; 18 Ami Parikh; 25 idreamphoto, (t) Sergey Popov V; 27(t) L.Watcharapoll;
29 Monika Wieland; 31(t) mikeledray; 32(bl) Janne Hamalainen; 33(br) Jakrit Jiraratwaro; 38 Christopher Meder;
39 Monika Wieland; 40(t) Andy.M; 44 joyfuldesigns; 45(tr) bright;
45(br) Moviestore Collection/Rex Features 46–47 holbox

All other photographs are from:
digitalSTOCK, digitalvision, PhotoAlto, PhotoDisc,

Every effort has been made to acknowledge the source and copyright holder of each picture.
Miles Kelly Publishing apologizes for any unintentional errors or omissions.

Made with paper from a sustainable forest

www.mileskelly.net

Contents

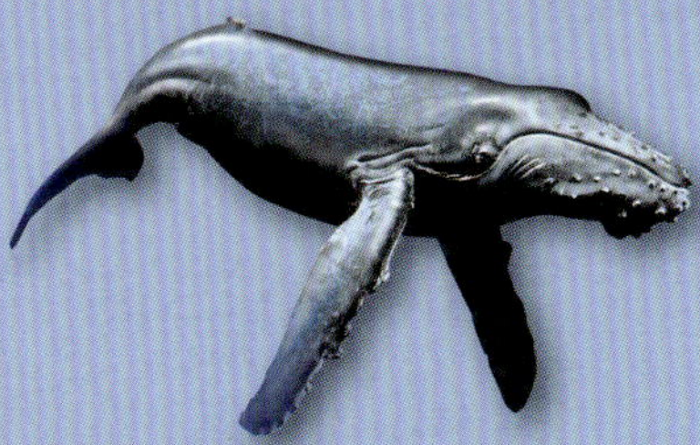

Marine mammals 6

The greatest animals 8

One big family 10

Inside whales and dolphins 12

Flippers, flukes and fins 14

Sensitive senses 16

Breathing and diving 18

Fierce hunters 20

Sieving the sea 22

Clicks, squeaks and squeals 24

Long-distance swimmers 26

Family of killers 28

Fast and sleek 30

River dolphins 32

Shy and secretive 34

Getting together 36

Whale and dolphin babies 38

Stories and mysteries 40

The old days of whaling 42

Working with people 44

Harm and help 46

Index 48

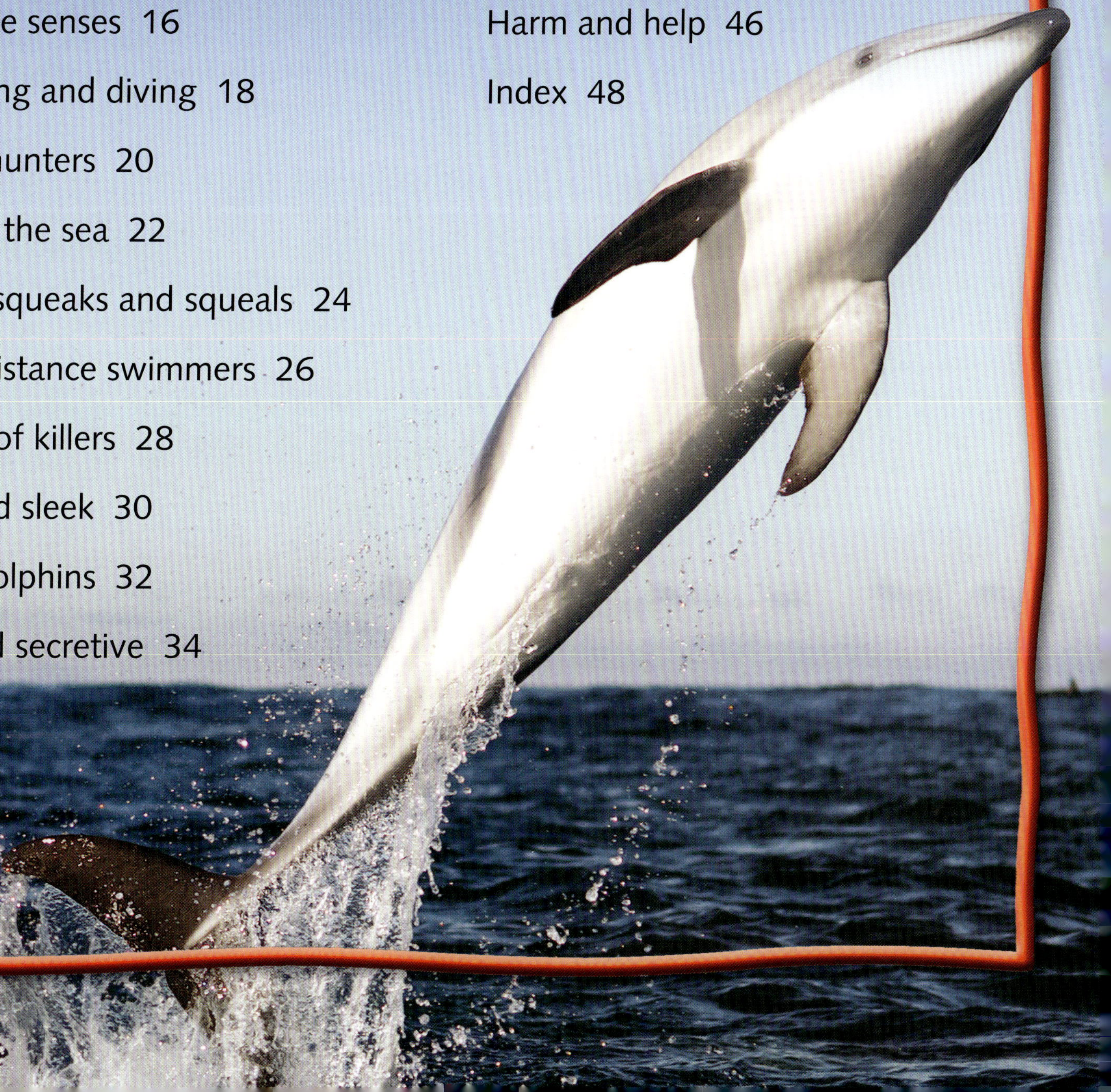

Marine mammals

1 **Whales, dolphins and porpoises are a fascinating group of marine animals also known as cetaceans.** Like other members of the mammal animal group, they have warm blood and breathe air. Almost all kinds live in the sea, apart from a few species of dolphin that live in freshwater rivers and lakes. This intelligent group holds many records – the biggest animal in the world, the largest hunter, and some of the fastest, deepest-diving creatures ever to have lived.

▶ Many kinds of dolphin live in groups called schools. Common dolphins are colourful, with yellow or tan patches along their sides and dark 'spectacles' around their eyes.

The greatest animals

2 **Whales are the biggest kind of animal alive today.** Some are longer and heavier than the largest trucks. They need lots of muscle power and energy to move their large bodies. As they live in the ocean, the water helps to support their huge bulk.

3 **The blue whale is the largest animal ever.** It can grow up to 30 metres in length, which is as long as seven cars placed end to end. It reaches up to 150 tonnes in weight – that's as heavy as 35 elephants.

▶ The blue whale is a true giant, as large as a submarine. Yet it is also gentle and swims slowly, unless frightened or injured.

4 On land, bears and tigers are the biggest hunting animals. However, the sperm whale is more than 100 times larger, making it the biggest predator (active hunter) on Earth. It grows up to 20 metres in length and 50 tonnes in weight.

TRUE OR FALSE?

1. The sperm whale is the biggest predator.
2. The blue whale weighs up to 30 tonnes.
3. Whales breathe oxygen through gills.

Answers:
1. True 2. False, it can weigh up to 150 tonnes 3. False

5 The animal with the largest mouth is the bowhead whale. Its body is 18 metres long, and its mouth makes up almost one-third of its length. Fin whales are the second largest whales, at an impressive 26 metres long.

▼ Killer whales come to the surface and open their nostrils, called blowholes, to breathe. They then dive back into the water again. The blowholes stay closed underwater.

6 Whales breathe air, just like humans. They must hold their breath as they dive underwater to feed. A few of them, such as the bottlenose whale, can stay underwater for more than one hour. Most humans have trouble holding their breath for even one minute!

▶ Bottlenose dolphins swim underwater for long periods of time, searching for food. They must then return to the surface to take in oxygen.

One big family

7 The mammal group of cetaceans is made up of about 80 kinds of whale, dolphin and porpoise. The whale group is then divided into two main types – baleen whales and toothed whales.

▼ The sperm whale is the biggest of the toothed whales. It only seems to have teeth in its lower jaw because those in its upper jaw can barely be seen.

MAKE A DOLPHIN!
You will need:
paper   coloured pens or pencils
Draw a dolphin outline and colour it any pattern you like. You can name it after its colour, such as the pink-spotted dolphin. Or use your own name, like Claire's dolphin.

8 Baleen whales are the largest members of the cetacean group. They are often called great whales. The sei whale, for example, is about 16 metres long. Baleen whales catch food with long strips in their mouths called baleen, or whalebone.

9 Toothed whales catch prey with their sharp teeth. This subgroup includes sperm whales, beaked whales and pilot whales. One example is the beluga, or white whale. It is one of the noisiest whales, making clicks, squeaks and trills.

◀ The beluga lives in the cold waters of the Arctic and can grow up to 5 metres in length.

▼ The finless porpoise, with its blunt 'beak' and bulging forehead, is one of the smallest cetaceans at about 1.5 metres in length.

10 Another group is made up of beaked whales. These are medium-sized whales with long, beak-shaped mouths. There are about 20 kinds, but some are very rare and hardly ever seen. The shepherd's beaked whale, which is about 7 metres in length, has been seen fewer than 20 times.

11 There are six species of porpoise. They are usually quite small, at 2 metres or less in length. They have blunter, more rounded heads than dolphins. The finless porpoise, as its name suggests, has a smooth back with no fin.

▶ The dusky dolphin is very inquisitive and likes to swim and leap near boats, perhaps in the hope of being fed.

Back is a dusky blue-black colour

Grey patch from eye to the flipper

White underside

12 There are more than 35 kinds of dolphin. Most of them are 2 to 3 metres in length. They are fast swimmers and can often be seen leaping above the waves. The dusky dolphin is one of the highest leapers, twisting and somersaulting before it splashes back into the sea.

Inside whales and dolphins

13 Whales, dolphins and porpoises are mammals. They have the same parts inside their bodies as humans. These include bones to make up the skeleton, lots of muscles, a stomach to hold food, a heart to pump blood, and lungs to breathe air.

14 Most mammals have hair or fur. Whales, dolphins and porpoises are unusual because they have smooth, hairless skin to make them streamlined. Only a few hairs, mainly bristles, can be found around the eyes, nose and mouth.

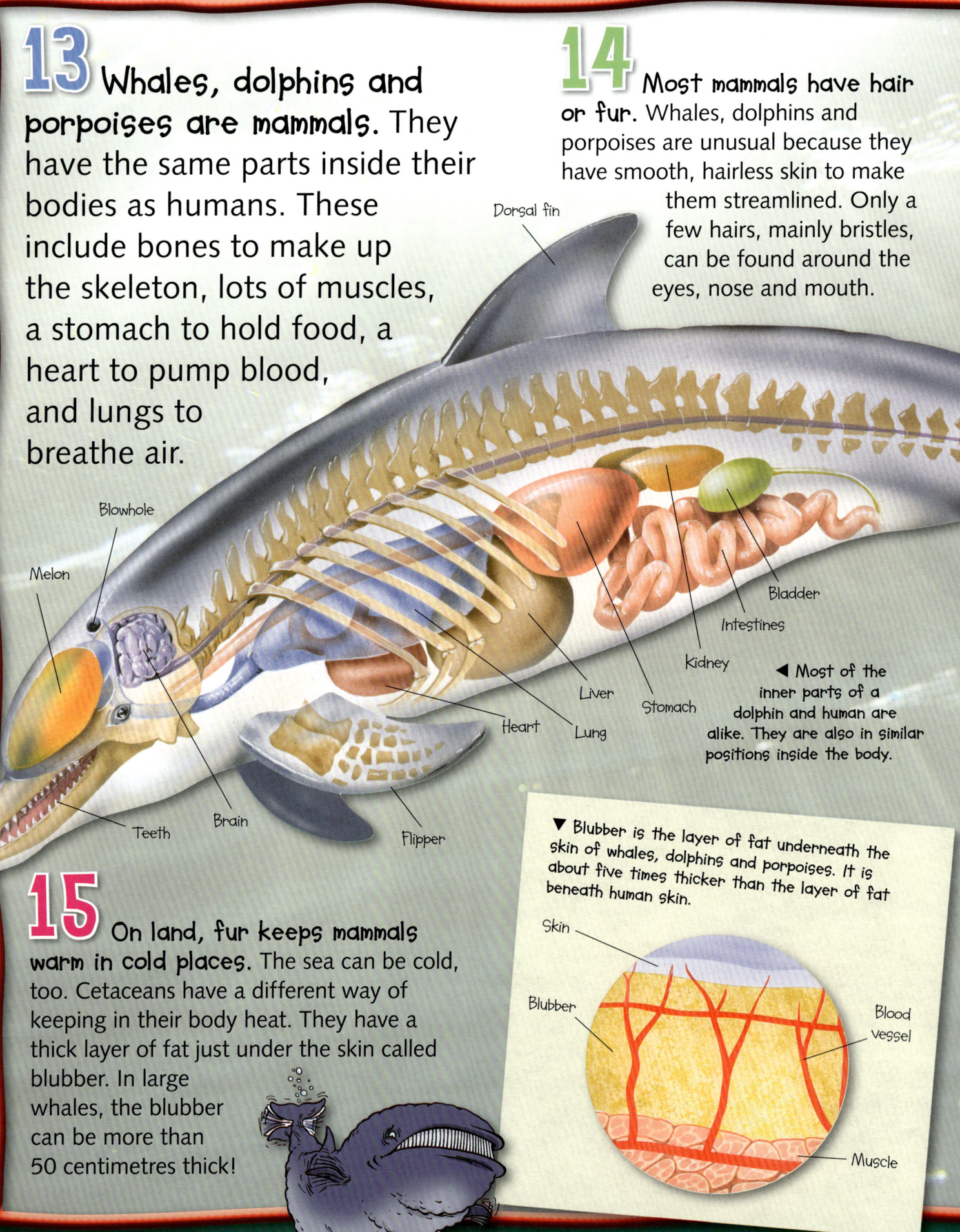

◀ Most of the inner parts of a dolphin and human are alike. They are also in similar positions inside the body.

▼ Blubber is the layer of fat underneath the skin of whales, dolphins and porpoises. It is about five times thicker than the layer of fat beneath human skin.

15 On land, fur keeps mammals warm in cold places. The sea can be cold, too. Cetaceans have a different way of keeping in their body heat. They have a thick layer of fat just under the skin called blubber. In large whales, the blubber can be more than 50 centimetres thick!

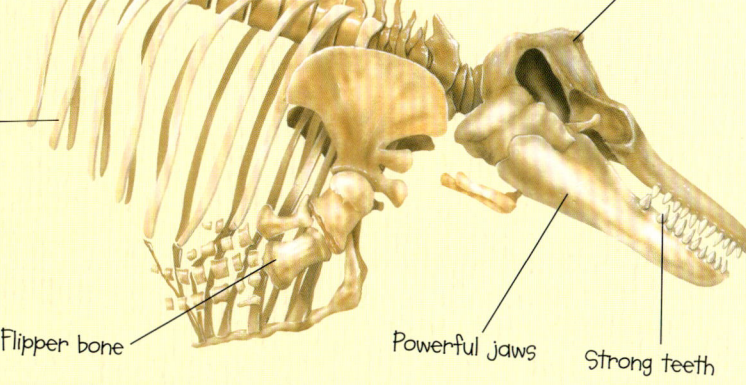

50–54 vertebrae (backbones), but no bones in the tail flukes

Skull

Barrel-shaped rib cage

Flipper bone

Powerful jaws

Strong teeth

▲ The skeleton of a whale or dolphin, such as this killer whale, is made up of bones. There are no rear leg bones and no bones in the dorsal fin (on the back) or in the tail flukes.

Fluke

16 Compared to most animals, whales, dolphins and porpoises have large brains for their size. Dolphins are clever creatures, able to learn tricks and solve simple puzzles. Some scientists believe that dolphins have even developed their own way of communicating.

17 Cetaceans often have small animals growing inside their bodies called parasites, such as lice. Parasites aren't needed for survival – the whale or dolphin provides them with food. Some baleen whales have their heads covered with barnacles (shellfish), which normally grow on seaside rocks.

▲ Barnacles are a type of shellfish. They stick firmly to large whales and cannot be rubbed off!

I DON'T BELIEVE IT!

The sperm whale has the biggest brain in the world. It weighs about 8 kilograms – that's over five times the size of a human brain. But its large brain does not mean it is the cleverest animal.

Flippers, flukes and fins

18 Most mammals have four legs and a tail. Instead, whales, dolphins and porpoises have flippers, a fin and a tail. Flippers are their front limbs, similar to human arms. In fact, flipper bones and human arm and hand bones are alike. Flippers are mainly used for swimming, scratching and waving to send messages to others in the group.

19 The tail of a cetacean is in two almost identical parts. Each part is called a fluke. Unlike the flippers, flukes have no bones. They are used for swimming as the body arches powerfully to swish them up and down. They can also be slapped onto the water's surface to send messages to other whales. This is called lobtailing.

▼ Whales can often be seen splashing backwards into the water. This is known as breaching. Even the huge humpback whale can breach — and it weighs more than 30 tonnes!

Flipper-slapping
Humpbacks wave their flippers in the air and splash them onto the surface

Lobtailing
When the tail is slapped onto the water's surface

MAKE A WHALE!

You will need:
long balloon   newspaper strips
paints   papier-mâché paste

Paste three layers of newspaper onto the balloon. Let it dry, then paint the whale and stick on paper fins and a tail.

20 Many whales, dolphins and porpoises jump out of the water. They then crash back down again with a big splash – this is called breaching. It may be done to send a loud message to others in the group, or to try and get rid of skin pests, such as barnacles and whale lice.

21 The fin on the back of many whales, dolphins and porpoises is known as a dorsal fin. In some, such as the killer whale, it is tall and narrow. In others, such as the bottlenose dolphin, it is shaped like a swept-back triangle. Blue whales have a tiny dorsal fin near the tail. Right whales, bowheads, belugas and narwhals have no dorsal fin at all.

Blue whale

Killer whale

Bottlenose dolphin

▲ Many whales, dolphins and porpoises can be recognized by their distinctive dorsal fin shapes.

Sensitive senses

22 Whales, dolphins and porpoises have many of the same senses as humans. Like us, they use sight and hearing, but because they live underwater these senses detect very different surroundings. A whale's eyes have adapted to cope with underwater conditions far better than a human's.

▼ Atlantic spotted dolphins roll over and rub each other. It's like saying, "Hello, we're in the same school."

23 One sense that humans don't have, but whales, dolphins and porpoises do is the ability to detect magnetism. Some whales may 'feel' the Earth's weak magnetic force, which humans would detect using a compass. This magnetic sense may help them to find their way on their long journeys, or migrations, through the wide and featureless ocean.

24 Whales, dolphins and porpoises have very sensitive skin, so the sense of touch is important to them. They rub and stroke others in their group, or a partner during breeding time. A mother whale often caresses her baby to provide comfort and warmth.

QUIZ

1. Do dolphins have a strong sense of smell?
2. Cetaceans use what word beginning with 'e' to sense objects?
3. Which sense do some whales use when migrating?

Answers:
1. No, it is very weak 2. Echolocation 3. Magnetic sense

25 Dolphins have a weak sense of smell, if any at all. Instead, they use their strong sense of taste to tell them about the foods they are eating. They can also taste the water. This lets them know what other bits of food might be drifting nearby.

26 Hearing is vital for whales, dolphins and porpoises. They don't have outer ears, like us. Instead, sounds in the water are detected inside the head. Many toothed whales find their way in dark water by making clicking sounds, then listening to the echoes that bounce off nearby objects. This method is called echolocation.

▶ Killer whales spyhop — look across the surface of the water — for the fins of others in their group or for signs of enemies, such as sharks.

Breathing and diving

27 Whales, dolphins and porpoises breathe air in and out of their lungs. They don't have gills to breathe underwater, like a fish, so they must hold their breath when diving. Air goes in and out of the body through the blowhole – a small opening on top of the head, just in front of the eyes. It works in a similar way to our nostrils.

▲ As a whale breathes out, its 'blow' often looks like a steamy fountain of water. It can be seen far away across the ocean – and on a calm day, it can be heard from a distance, too.

▶ A giant squid tries to escape a sperm whale. The largest giant squid ever caught by a sperm whale was 12 metres in length.

28 When a whale comes to the surface after a dive, it breathes out air hard and fast. The moist air, mixed with slimy mucus from the whale's breathing passages, turns into water droplets. This makes the whale's breath look like a jet of steam or a fountain. It's called the 'blow'. All whales have 'blows' of different size and shape. This can help to identify them when they are hidden underwater.

29 Many cetaceans feed near the surface, so do not need to dive more than 50 metres down. The champion diver is the sperm whale. It can go down more than 3000 metres to hunt its prey of giant squid.

30 Most dolphins and porpoises dive and hold their breath for one or two minutes. Large whales can stay underwater for a longer period of time, perhaps for 15 to 20 minutes. The sperm whale can dive for more than two hours!

① The sperm whale surfaces and breathes in and out powerfully several times

② It then straightens out its body and may disappear beneath the surface

③ The whale then reappears and begins to arch its back

④ By arching its back and tipping its head downwards, the whale prepares to dive

⑤ Its tail is lifted out of the water as it begins to dive

⑥ The sperm whale dives deep into the darkness of the ocean

▶ The sperm whale is one of the greatest diving whales and may perform this sequence each time it dives to the cold, dark depths of the ocean.

Fierce hunters

31 **Dolphins, porpoises and toothed whales are active hunting carnivores.** They eat meat – the flesh of sea creatures, especially fish and squid. Some of them crunch up hard-shelled crabs, shrimps and prawns, or shellfish, such as oysters and whelks.

32 **Beaked whales mainly eat squid.** In some species, males have just two or four teeth, which look like tusks. Females have none at all. These whales suck in their prey and swallow it whole.

33 **A typical dolphin has 60 to 100 teeth.** They are in pairs, left and right, in the upper and lower jaws. These teeth are not usually thin and sharp like fangs, but wide and cone-shaped. The teeth are the same shape all along the jaw, unlike the teeth of a cat, dog or human. This is the best design for catching their slippery food.

▲ Dolphins swim around small fish that gather into a tight group called a 'bait-ball'. Then the dolphins dash into the bait-ball and try to grab the fish. From above shearwater seabirds divebomb the bait-ball as well.

▶ This bottlenose dolphin has found a tasty octopus to eat.

34 Most dolphins and porpoises chase their speedy prey. They quickly twist and turn in the water, snapping at victims. Once a dolphin catches its prey, it flicks it back into its mouth and swallows it whole. With a larger victim, the dolphin bites off a big chunk and swallows it. Whales, dolphins and porpoises hardly ever chew their food.

35 The sperm whale has about 50 teeth in its lower jaw, which are about 20 centimetres in length. The teeth in its upper jaw are so tiny, they can barely be seen.

QUIZ!
1. Do sperm whales have large teeth in their upper or lower jaw?
2. Are dolphins vegetarians?
3. What word beginning with 'b' describes a tight group of fish swimming together?

Answers:
1. Lower jaw 2. No, they are meat-eaters 3. Bait-ball

Sieving the sea

36 Great whales are also called baleen whales because of the baleen in their mouths. Baleen is sometimes known as whalebone, but it is not bone. It's a light, tough and springy substance, like plastic. It hangs down in long strips from the whale's upper jaw. Baleen varies in size depending on the whale species.

▲ The bowhead whale's baleen hangs like a huge curtain, big enough for ten people to hide behind.

37 Most baleen whales, such as the blue, fin and sei, cruise-feed. This means that they feed by swimming slowly through a swarm of shrimp-like creatures called krill with their mouths open.

38 As a baleen whale feeds, it takes in a huge mouthful of water — enough to fill more than 100 bathtubs! This makes the skin around its throat expand like a balloon. The whale's food, such as krill, is in the water. The whale pushes the water out between the baleen plates. The baleen's bristles catch the krill like a giant filter. Then the whale licks off the krill and swallows them.

Baleen

39 **The humpback whale makes a 'bubble curtain' to catch krill.** It dives down, then swims up slowly in small circles as it breathes out. The bubbles created rise quickly and form a tube-shaped curtain that keeps the krill, or other food, close together in a bait-ball. Then the humpback moves in to feed with its mouth open wide.

▲ When grey whales scoop up food from the seabed they can leave deep grooves like a ploughed field.

40 **The grey whale often feeds on the shallow seabed.** It swims on one side and drags its mouth through the mud. Then it pushes the water and mud out of its mouth. This traps food in its baleen, such as shellfish and shrimps.

◀ Humpback whales feed by rising up through shoals of fish with their mouths open and throat skin bulging. They scoop up water, push it out through the baleen and eat the food left inside their mouths.

I DON'T BELIEVE IT!
In summer, the blue whale eats 4 tonnes of food in one day! That's about four million krill. In winter, it eats hardly anything for many weeks because food is scarce.

Clicks, squeaks and squeals

41 Whales, dolphins and porpoises can be very noisy animals. They make loud clicks and whistles to help them navigate, hunt prey and communicate with each other. These noises travel long distances underwater, so divers can often hear them. Some whale noises can be heard more than 100 kilometres away.

42 Sounds are especially important for detecting objects by echolocation. The dolphin detects the returning echoes of its own clicks. It can then work out the size and shape of objects nearby – whether a rock, coral, a shipwreck or a shoal of fish.

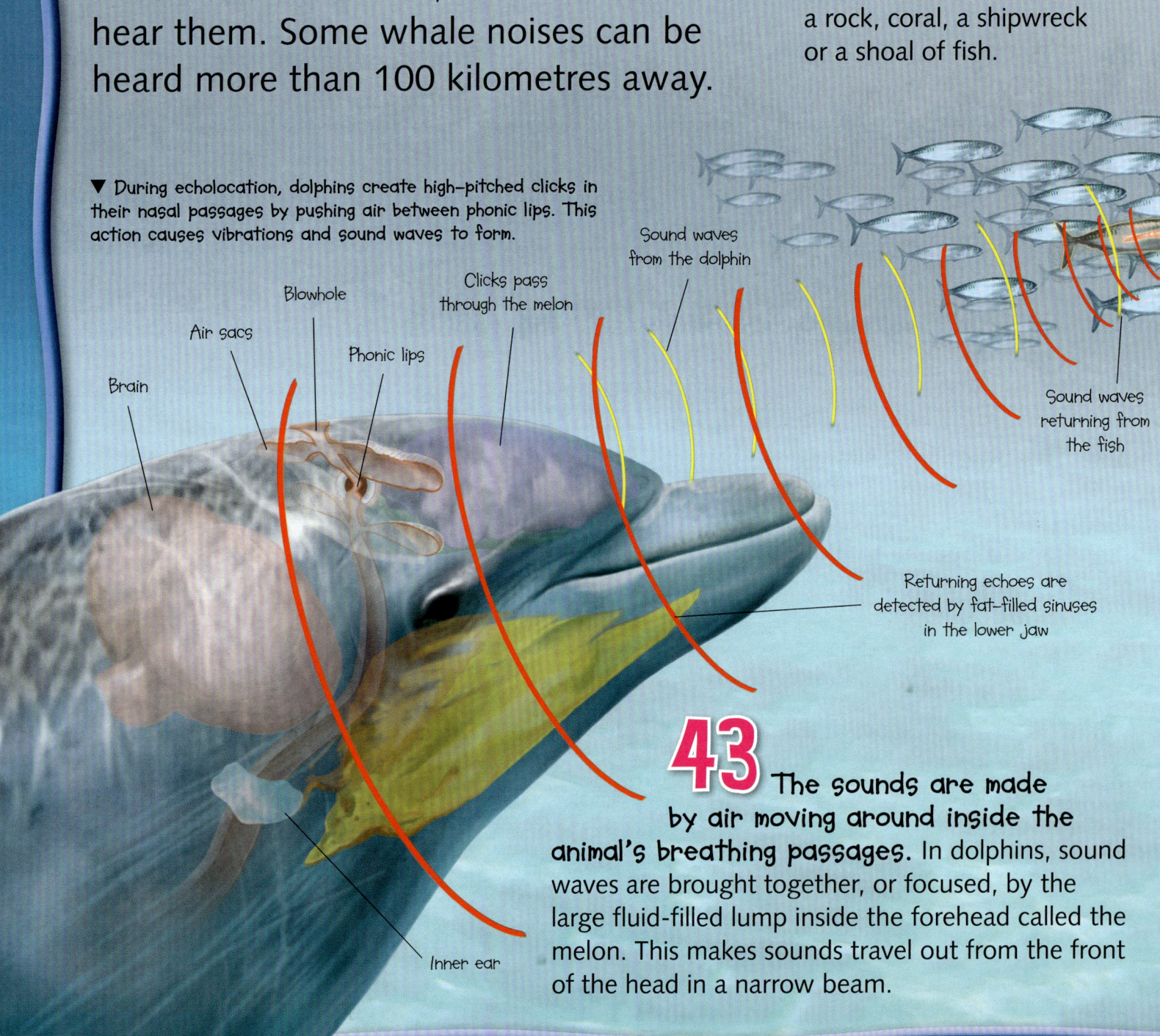

▼ During echolocation, dolphins create high-pitched clicks in their nasal passages by pushing air between phonic lips. This action causes vibrations and sound waves to form.

Brain
Air sacs
Blowhole
Phonic lips
Clicks pass through the melon
Sound waves from the dolphin
Sound waves returning from the fish
Returning echoes are detected by fat-filled sinuses in the lower jaw
Inner ear

43 The sounds are made by air moving around inside the animal's breathing passages. In dolphins, sound waves are brought together, or focused, by the large fluid-filled lump inside the forehead called the melon. This makes sounds travel out from the front of the head in a narrow beam.

44 **Sounds are also used for communication.** Belugas and dolphins especially make a vast range of clicks, squeals and squeaks. Sounds help them to stay together in their groups, and to work together when hunting fish.

◀ Scientists think that dolphins may use sound to identify other members of their pod.

◀ This whale is about to slap the surface of the water with its fluke. This is one way whales make noises with their bodies to talk to each other.

45 **Scientists have spent time closely watching dolphins to see if they use a language to communicate.** Certain sounds seem to occur more often when dolphins are resting, swimming, playing, feeding or breeding.

MAKE DOLPHIN NOISES
You will need:
sheet of card   ruler   plastic comb

Roll the card into a funnel and squeal through the narrow end. Rub the teeth of the comb along a ruler to produce dolphin-like clicks.

Long-distance swimmers

▲ Baleen whales, such as the humpback, make long journeys so that they can give birth in tropical waters. Then the baby is able to grow stronger in calm waters before migrating to colder areas.

46 Many cetaceans migrate (go on long journeys) to find food at the same time each year. Baleen whales spend summer in cold northern or southern waters where there are vast amounts of food. For winter they swim back to the tropics. Although there is little food there, the water is warm and calm.

47 Baleen whales usually swim in groups as they migrate. They can often be seen 'spyhopping'. This means they swing around into an upright position, lift their heads above the water and turn slowly to look all around as they sink back into the water. This is especially common in whales that migrate along coasts.

I DON'T BELIEVE IT!
The migration of the grey whale takes less than six weeks. It would take a strong swimmer 30 weeks to complete the same journey.

In summer, grey whales swim back to the coast of Alaska to feed

48 **The grey whale makes the longest migration of any whale — and mammal.** In spring, grey whales swim from their breeding areas in the subtropical waters around the coast of Mexico. They head north along the west coast of North America to the Arctic Ocean for summer feeding. In autumn, they return in the opposite direction.

In winter, the whales travel south to Mexico to have babies

▲ Grey whales travel up to 20,000 kilometres every year, between the icy Arctic region and warm subtropical waters.

49 **Belugas and narwhals migrate from the cold waters of the southern area of the Arctic Ocean to the even icier waters further north!** They follow the edge of the ice sheet as it shrinks and melts back each spring, then grows again each autumn.

◀ This conservation worker is fitting a satellite transmitter to a Beluga whale to keep track of its movements as it migrates.

50 **Many cetaceans can now be tracked by satellite.** A radio beacon is fixed, usually to the dorsal fin, and its signals are picked up by satellites in space. This shows that some whales complete exactly the same migration every year, while others wander far more widely around the oceans.

Family of killers

51 All cetaceans are carnivores, meaning they eat various kinds of animal as food. The killer whale can kill and eat almost any creature in the sea, from a small fish to a large whale. It is also known as the orca. It is not actually a whale, but the biggest member of the dolphin family.

52 Killer whales live in oceans all over the world. Their black-and-white markings make them easy to recognize. Males grow up to 9 metres in length and 10 tonnes in weight. They have tall, slim, triangular fins up to 2 metres in height. Females are slightly smaller and have lower, more rounded fins.

▼ A killer whale suddenly appears out of the surf and tries to grab an unsuspecting sea lion before it has time to escape.

▲ Cruising killer whales are constantly on the lookout for food. They listen and feel for splashes that may indicate nearby prey.

53 **Killer whales live in groups called pods.** A pod is like a big family. Normally, there are 20 to 30 whales in a pod. Older females are usually in charge. Throughout the year, the females decide where to travel, where to rest and when the pod will hunt.

54 **Members of a killer whale pod communicate by making noises, such as clicks and grunts.** They work together to surround a shoal of fish, such as tuna. The killer whale also feeds by 'surfing' onto a beach and grabbing a young seal or sea lion. Then the whale wriggles back into the sea, holding its victim by its sharp, back-curved teeth.

MAKE AN ORCA POD!

You will need:
white card   scissors   sticky tape
black pen   cotton thread

Draw and cut out killer whales of different sizes. Thread cotton through a small hole in the fin of all but the biggest whale. Then, dangle each whale from the larger whale by taping them to its body.

Fast and sleek

55 **Dolphins are fast, active swimmers.** They always seem to be looking for things to do, food to eat and friends to play with. They range in size from Commerson's dolphins, which are only 2 metres in length, to bottlenose dolphins, which are double the size at about 4 metres in length.

57 **Spinner dolphins are well known for their spectacular leaps high into the air.** Many dolphins somersault as they leap, but spinners twist and spin around as well, five or more times in each leap. They don't seem to mind if they land on their side, tail or head, and leap out to do it again.

56 **Many dolphins like to bow-ride.** This means riding in the bow wave of a ship or boat – the v-shaped wave made by the boat's sharp front end slicing through the water. Exactly why they do this is not clear. They may be waiting for leftover food to be thrown from the boat.

▶ This playful bottlenose dolphin is bow-riding. It may be saving energy by 'surfing' in the ship's wave.

I DON'T BELIEVE IT!
The long tusk-like tooth of the narwhal was once sold as the 'real horn' of the mythical horse, the unicorn.

▲ Dolphins are highly social animals that often live in large groups. This school of dolphins is swimming, leaping and diving through the waves.

58 **Dolphins are often seen swimming in large groups.** Several kinds of dolphin sometimes form even bigger groups of many thousands. Pantropical spotted dolphins form huge groups and are very active – leaping and swimming. From a distance, the sea can look like it is boiling!

59 **Striped dolphins are some of the fastest swimmers.** They live in all oceans, in groups of up to 3000. Striped dolphins often jump clear of the water in long, low leaps as they swim at speed. This is called 'porpoising', even when dolphins do it!

▲ The divers on this inflatable boat have a spectacular view of two dolphins leaping. Dolphins can reach fast speeds as they dart through the water.

River dolphins

60 Several kinds of dolphin only live in rivers or lakes. Most are rare and face many risks. They include pollution, injury from the propellers of ships, and becoming trapped in fishing nets. Other dangers include being caught as food for humans, or starvation because humans have overfished rivers and lakes.

▼ The Amazon River in South America provides the freshwater habitat (home) for the boto.

▶ As the boto comes to the surface and breathes out, the noise it produces sounds like a human sighing.

61 The boto, or Amazon River dolphin, lives in several rivers in South America. It has a very long, slim, beak-like mouth and grows to about 2 metres in length. It feeds mainly in the early morning and late evening. By day it rests floating on its side, waving one flipper in the air. When the Amazon rainforest floods in the wet season, the boto swims among the huge trees.

QUIZ

Can you match these river dolphins to their native countries?

1. Boto
2. Baiji
3. Indus River dolphin

A. China
B. Brazil
C. India

Answers:
1.B 2.A 3.C

62 **The World Conservation Union (IUCN) has classified one of Asia's river dolphins as critically endangered.** The baiji, or Yangtze dolphin of China, is probably extinct – a survey in 2006 failed to find any specimens in the wild. Two other species, the Indus and Ganges River dolphins, live in Indian rivers. They are grey-brown in colour and grow to about 2 metres in length.

◀ The extinct Yangtze dolphin had a white underside and a pale blue-grey back.

▶ One of the main causes of the baiji's probable extinction is the pollution of the Yangtze, by factories along its banks and by farm chemicals seeping into the water.

63 **Two kinds of dolphin live in both rivers and the sea, usually staying close to the shore.** One is the tucuxi, which is quite small at just 1.5 metres in length. It can be found in the Amazon River and around the northeast coast of South America. The other is the Irrawaddy dolphin, found in the seas and rivers of Southeast Asia, from India to northern Australia. It has a blunt nose and blue-grey skin.

64 **The franciscana or La Plata dolphin is a river dolphin that has gone back to the sea.** It is similar to river dolphins, but lives in shallow water along the southeast coasts of South America. It can be recognized by its very long, slim, sword-like beak.

Shy and secretive

65 Porpoises are in a different subgroup to whales and dolphins. There are six species that are all found in the sea. Most live in shallow water near to coasts and shores. Porpoises have spade-shaped teeth, whereas dolphins have cone-shaped teeth.

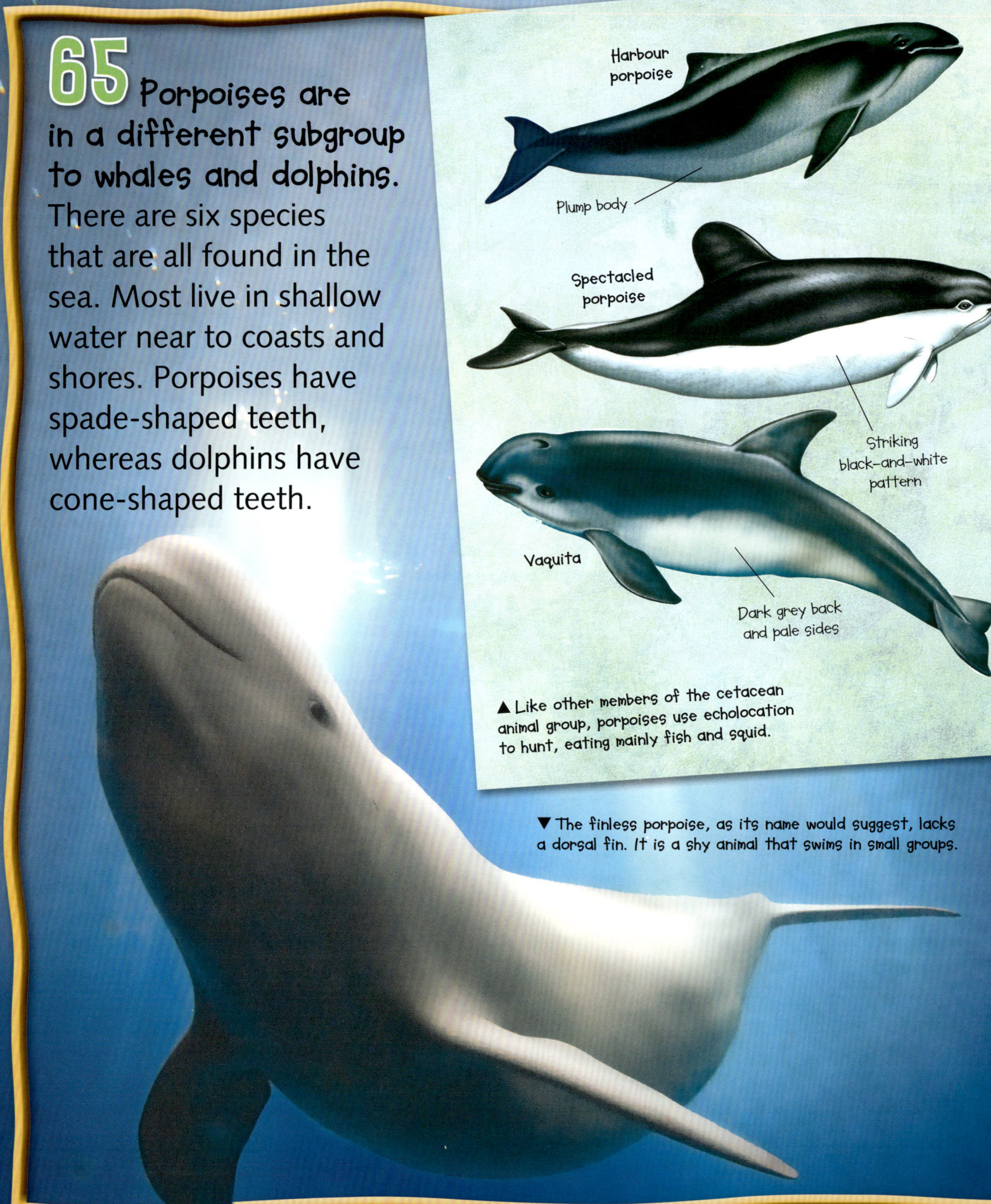

Harbour porpoise — Plump body

Spectacled porpoise — Striking black-and-white pattern

Vaquita — Dark grey back and pale sides

▲ Like other members of the cetacean animal group, porpoises use echolocation to hunt, eating mainly fish and squid.

▼ The finless porpoise, as its name would suggest, lacks a dorsal fin. It is a shy animal that swims in small groups.

QUIZ

You're at the beach and you see a stranded whale, do you...

A. Run away and keep quiet
B. Find an adult, and contact the police or coastguard
C. Sing the whale a song

Answer: B

66 **The spectacled porpoise has a black ring, surrounded by a white ring, around each eye.** It can be found in the Southern Ocean around the lower tip of South America, and near islands such as the Falklands and South Georgia.

67 **The harbour or common porpoise is familiar to sailors around the northern waters.** It has the nickname 'puffing pig' because its blow is rarely seen, but can be heard as a series of loud, short puffs – like a mixture of a snort and a sneeze. It eats a wide range of food, including leftovers thrown from boats.

▲ When Dall's porpoise swims quickly through water, a long, narrow spray spurts along its back. It is known as the 'rooster's tail' due to its shape.

68 **Dall's porpoise is the largest of the group, at about 2 metres long and 200 kilograms in weight.** It lives along the shores of the North Pacific Ocean. It's a fast and agile swimmer, dashing along at over 50 kilometres an hour. However, it rarely leaps above the surface of the water like other porpoises.

Getting together

69 Whales, dolphins and porpoises breed like most other mammals. A male and female get together and mate. The female becomes pregnant and a baby develops inside her womb. The baby is born through her birth canal, a small opening near her tail.

71 Baleen whales have babies to fit in with their long journeys, or migrations. They give birth in the tropics, where the water is warm all year. This gives the new baby time to grow and become stronger in warm, calm seas, before the migration to colder waters for summer feeding.

70 When a male and female get together, it is called courtship. They need to find a partner so they can have babies, otherwise they would eventually die out. For hours, they swim together and stroke each other with their flippers and flukes. They may also make noises, like 'love songs'. One of the most amazing is the song of the male humpback whale. He travels through the water making wails, squeals and shrieks in a repeating pattern that lasts for up to 22 hours. Then after a pause, he does it again – just to attract a partner!

SWORD FIGHT

You will need:
straws   bucket of water   blue food dye

Put the food dye in the water. Hold a straw end in each hand, put your hands just under the surface, making the straws poke out above. Now start 'fencing' – like two male narwhals having a swordfight.

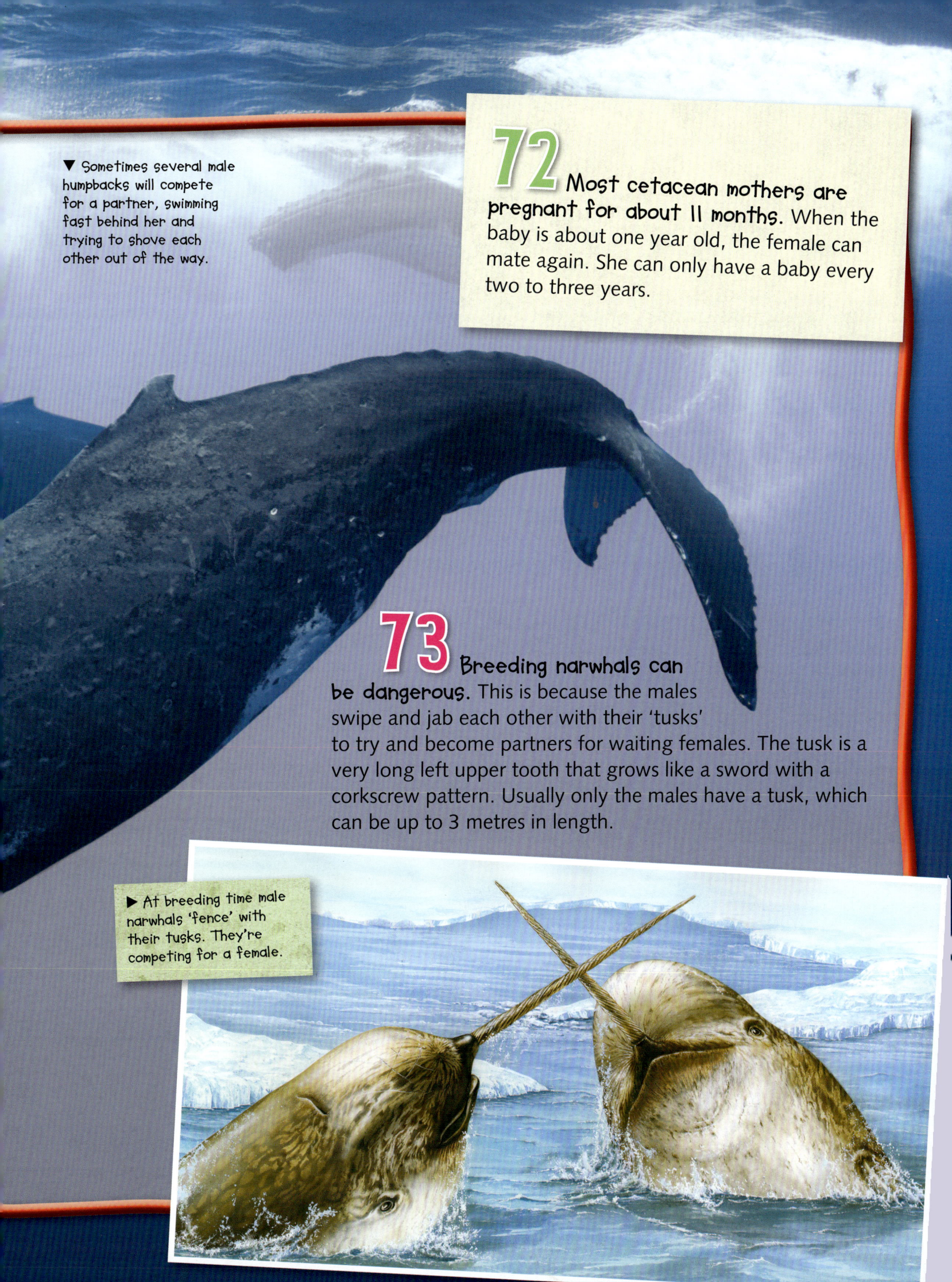

▼ Sometimes several male humpbacks will compete for a partner, swimming fast behind her and trying to shove each other out of the way.

72 Most cetacean mothers are pregnant for about 11 months. When the baby is about one year old, the female can mate again. She can only have a baby every two to three years.

73 Breeding narwhals can be dangerous. This is because the males swipe and jab each other with their 'tusks' to try and become partners for waiting females. The tusk is a very long left upper tooth that grows like a sword with a corkscrew pattern. Usually only the males have a tusk, which can be up to 3 metres in length.

▶ At breeding time male narwhals 'fence' with their tusks. They're competing for a female.

Whale and dolphin babies

74 Most female whales, dolphins and porpoises have one baby at a time. Twins or more are very rare. The baby, called a calf, is usually born tail first. It needs to start breathing air at once. The mother nudges it up to the surface of the water, so it can gasp its first breaths.

▲ This tiny newborn dolphin calf is swimming closely alongside its mother for safety.

75 A new baby stays very close to its mother. She protects it, charging at enemies, such as sharks, large sea lions and seals – and perhaps killer whales.

▼ The young beluga is born dark grey or pinky-grey. It gradually becomes lighter, but it may not take on its all-white colouration until it is more than five years old. This calf is about to suckle milk from its mother.

76 Like other mammals, the mother feeds her baby on her own milk. It is very rich and full of goodness. The calf sucks it from the mother's teat, which is usually hidden under a fold of skin on her underside.

77 Most baby cetaceans feed on their mother's milk for about one year. They grow quickly and soon become strong swimmers. Their mothers teach them how to hunt. By 18 to 24 months of age, the young are independent – able to look after themselves. Baby baleen whales feed on their mother's milk for less time, for only 6 to 8 months.

▼ A female killer whale gives birth to one calf at a time. The mother and baby stay close together until the calf is weaned off its mother's milk.

I DON'T BELIEVE IT!

The blue whale calf is the world's biggest baby at 7 metres in length and 3 tonnes in weight. It drinks 350 litres of its mother's milk everyday – enough to fill four bathtubs!

78 It is difficult to know how long whales, dolphins and porpoises live. Scientists can guess their age from the way their teeth grow. Inside the teeth of some species are rings, like the rings in tree trunks. On average, there is one ring for each year of growth. Most dolphins survive for 15 to 25 years. Baleen whales may live for 70 to 80 years. However, some whales and dolphins have been known to survive much longer.

Stories and mysteries

▲ Common dolphins are pictured on the walls of the palaces at Knossos in Crete, which were built by the Minoans about 4000 years ago.

79 **Thousands of years ago cetaceans were greatly admired.** The ancient Greeks and Minoans created pictures and statues of them in their palaces and temples. Whale bones and carvings have been found in the remains of settlements that are 4000 years old, from the Inuits of North America and the Norse people of Northern Europe.

80 **Whales and dolphins feature in many songs, tales and books.** In the Bible, Jonah was swallowed by a whale. Rudyard Kipling wrote a story called *How the Whale Got Its Throat* to explain why the whale has grooves on its throat.

81 *Moby Dick*, **written by Herman Melville in 1851, is one of the best-known whale stories.** It is an adventure tale about Captain Ahab's quest to catch and kill a huge white sperm whale called Moby Dick because it had injured him.

▼ In the novel *Moby Dick*, the giant whale ferociously fights off the sailors who try to hunt him.

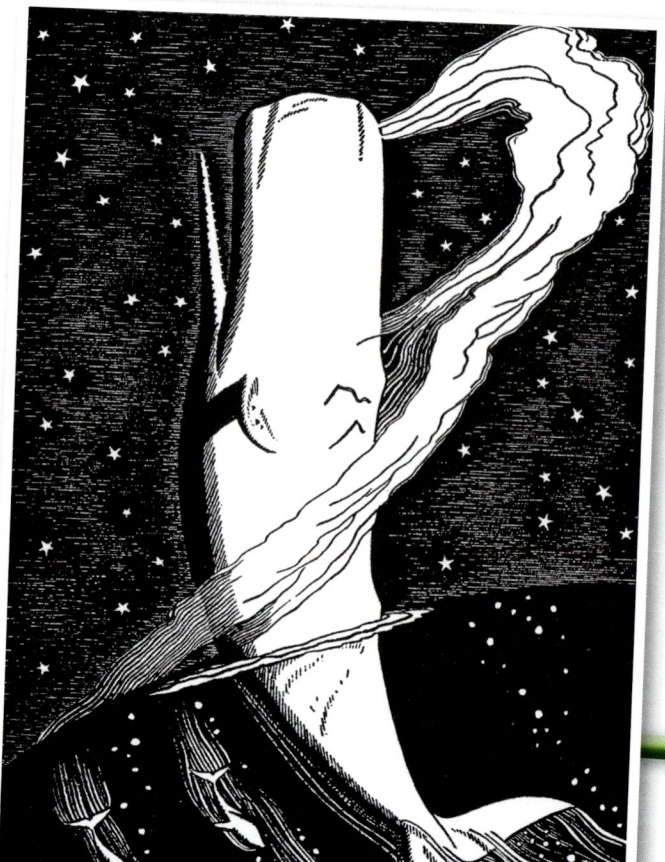

40

QUIZ

1. Which whale species is often found stranded?
2. On which Greek island are the ancient palaces at Knossos?
3. What type of whale is Moby Dick in Herman Melville's novel of the same name?

Answers:
1. Pilot whales 2. Crete 3. Sperm whale

82 No one knows for sure why cetaceans can become stranded on shores. Scientists have come up with possible reasons – the animals may be ill, or may have been disturbed by storms or undersea earthquakes. Or they may simply be lost, looking for a way to escape predators.

83 Among the most common victims of stranding are pilot whales. They live in close groups and have strong bonds with each other. If one whale strays too near the shore, it may become stranded. Other members of the group will often follow it because they don't want to leave the stranded whale alone. They then become stuck on the shore, too. Sometimes more than 50 pilot whales end up stranded.

◀ These people are trying to rescue some stranded pilot whales. It is a tricky task that needs skill and knowledge, and sometimes specialized equipment.

The old days of whaling

84 About 1000 years ago, the Basque people from northern Spain began to hunt whales from boats. The hunting spread around Europe, across the Atlantic to North America, then to southern regions like South Africa. By the early 1800s, hundreds of sailing ships were whaling every day. The men used small rowing boats and spears.

▼ In this early 19th-century scene, off the Atlantic coast of North America, a harpooner takes aim at a right whale from his rowing boat. The main hunting boat approaches in the distance.

85 In the mid 1800s, the harpoon gun was invented. It used explosives to fire a harpoon tied to a strong rope, so the whale could be hauled back. Steamships replaced old sailing ships. They could travel further and faster in most weather conditions. The mass slaughter of whales began.

86 By the mid 1900s, whaling fleets were large and well equipped. Catcher boats pursued and harpooned the whales. Their bodies were hauled onto a giant factory ship for processing. However by this time, many areas of the ocean had no whales left. They had all been killed.

87 **Whales were used in many ways.** Their fat, oil and blubber went into foods such as margarines, and was burned in lamps. The meat was eaten in some areas, especially eastern Asia. The baleen was used in machinery and for fashion items, such as women's corsets.

88 **During the 1970s, people around the world began to turn against whaling.** It seemed cruel to spear and kill these mammals. Also, many kinds of whale were so rare, they were in danger of being killed off completely.

▲ Whale bones were once used as building materials and tools to make glue and fertilizer.

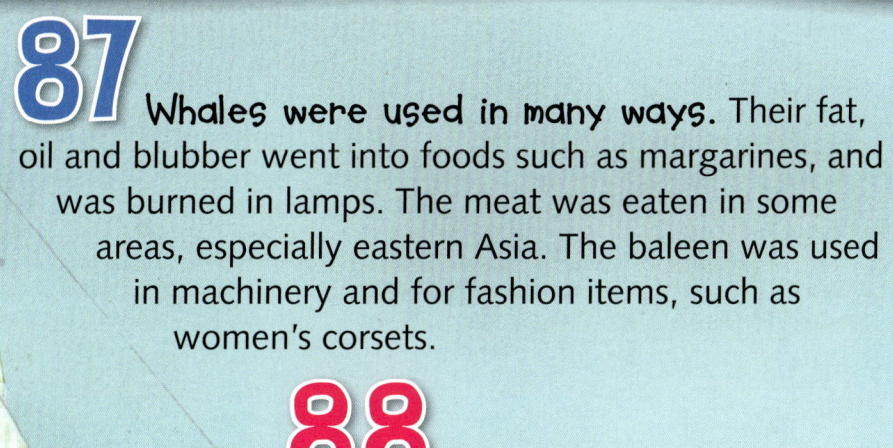

89 **The International Whaling Commission controls the whaling industry.** In 1986, it decided to ban mass slaughter of whales, with an international agreement, or moratorium.

90 **Some whales have now returned to areas where they had been killed off.** Whales breed slowly – females only have one baby every two or three years – so it will take a long time until whales are plentiful in the oceans again.

Working with people

91 **Many people visit an aquarium or sea-life centre to see whales, dolphins and porpoises.** The most common cetacean kept in captivity is the bottlenose dolphin. Some centres have killer whales and a few even have minke whales. Although they are the smallest of the baleen group, minke whales can still grow up to 10 metres long and 10 tonnes in weight.

WHAT A PERFORMANCE!

You will need:
thick card   scissors   pens or crayons
drinking straw   sticky tape

Draw, cut out and colour a dolphin outline on card. Stick the straw to it, as a handle. Now invent tricks and put on your own show.

92 **Dolphins can be interesting creatures to work with.** Trainers are able to build a strong bond with them. Dolphins even change tricks or invent new puzzles to make them more fun.

▼ Dolphins can be trained by professionals to perform tricks in return for food. They can learn to leap through hoops and knock balls with their beaks.

▼ At the Dolphin Research Institute in Hawaii, US, researchers study dolphin intelligence. This clever dolphin has correctly recognized a shape it was shown a few minutes before. It indicates its answer by pressing the nearest paddle with its beak.

93 Dolphins are very clever creatures. Studies performed on dolphins in captivity have shown that they are able to correctly recognize shapes and even count.

94 Some people believe all captive dolphins should be set free. The dolphins are sometimes kept in small, bare tanks, with few toys. They may take part in several shows each day and can get bored and tired. They may suffer from loneliness or illness.

95 There are arguments in favour of captive dolphins, too. If several animals live together in a big, safe pool, with plenty of equipment and good food they shouldn't get bored. Spectators can see what amazing animals they are, and learn more about saving wild dolphins.

▲ Free Willy (1993) told the tale of a boy's quest to set free a performing killer whale. The killer whale that starred in the film was released into the sea near Norway.

Harm and help

96 **Most baleen whales are protected by law around the world.** Only a small amount of controlled hunting is allowed, although illegal hunting continues in some countries. Conservation parks, such as the Southern Sanctuary in Antarctica, are set aside to protect marine life.

▲ Pilot whales can be found in groups. Unfortunately this makes it easier for whale hunters to catch them.

97 **Despite these laws, hunting of whales, dolphins and porpoises still goes on.** Some whalers have turned to catching smaller types, such as melon-headed whales and pilot whales. If the hunting continues, they may also face extinction.

98 **Whales and dolphins can drown even though they live in water.** If they get stuck underwater for some reason, they cannot breathe and may die. One of the greatest dangers for cetaceans is becoming trapped in fishing nets – this causes nearly 1000 to die each day.

▼ This humpback whale is being released back into the ocean after being caught and tangled in a fishing line.

I DON'T BELIEVE IT!

There are stories of people being saved by dolphins when in danger at sea. The dolphin may nudge them to shore. Some people even tell of dolphins protecting them from sharks!

99 Another hazard for cetaceans is pollution. Chemicals from coastal factories, power stations and oil refineries wash along rivers into the sea. Some dolphins, especially river dolphins, and porpoises are badly affected because they live near to the shore.

100 Ecotourism is becoming popular. Tourists take trips on whale-watching boats, or swim with dolphins near the beach. The money made should be used to support wildlife and conservation. In some places this does not happen, and the whales and dolphins are disturbed or frightened. It's a delicate balance between our use of the sea and its creatures, and looking after their environment and well-being.

▼ This group of tourists get an incredible view of a majestic humpback whale breaching near Hawaii.

Index

Entries in **bold** refer to main subject entries. Entries in *italics* refer to illustrations.

A
anatomy 12, *12*, *24*
Amazon River dolphin 32, *32*
Atlantic spotted dolphin *16–17*

B
baiji (river dolphin) 33, *33*
bait-balls *20–21*, 23
baleen 10, 22, *22*, 43
baleen whales 10, 13, **22–23**, *22–23*, 26, *26*, 36, 39, 44, 46
barnacles 13, *13*, 15
beaked whales 10, 11, 20
beluga whale 10, 15, 25, 27, *27*, 38, *38*
blowholes 9, *9*, 18
blubber 12, *12*, 43
blue whale 8, *8*, 15, *15*, 22
boto (river dolphin) 32, *32*
bottlenose dolphin 15, *15*, *21*, 30, *30*, 44
bow-riding 30, *30*
bowhead whale 9, 15, 22, *22*
breaching *14–15*, 15
breathing 9, *9*, 12, **18–19**, *18*, 38
breeding 16, **36–37**, 43
'bubble curtain' 23

C
calves (babies) 16, 26, 36, 37, **38–39**, *38*, *39*
captivity **44–45**
Commerson's dolphin 30
common dolphin 6, *6*, 40, *40*
common porpoise 34, 35
communication 13, 14, 15, 24, 25, 29
conservation 46, 47
courtship **36–37**

D
Dall's porpoise 35, *35*
diving 6, 18–19, *19*, 23
dusky dolphin 11, *11*

E
echolocation 17, 24, *24*, 34
ecotourism 47
eyesight 16

F
feeding 19, **20–21**, **22–23**, 26, 29, 35, 38–39
fin whale 9, 22
finless porpoise 11, *11*, 34
fins **14–15**, *15*, 27, 28
flippers 14, 32
Free Willy 45

G
Ganges River dolphin 33
great whales *see* baleen whales
grey whale 23, *23*, 27

H
harbour porpoise 34, *34*, 35
hazards 32, **42–43**, **46–47**
hearing 17
humpback whale *14–15*, 23, *22–23*, 26, 36, *36–37*, 46, 47
hunting 19, **20–21**, 24, 25, 28, 29, 39

I
Indus River dolphin 33
intelligence 13, 44, 45
Irrawaddy dolphin 33

K
killer whale 9, *9*, 13, *13*, 15, *15*, 17, **28–29**, *28*, *29*, 38, 39, *39*, 45
krill 22, 23

L
La Plata dolphin 33
leaping 11, 30, 31, *31*
lifespan 39
lobtailing 14, *14*

M
magnetic sense 16
mammals 6, 12, 38
melon *12*, 24, *24*
melon-headed whale 46
migration 16, **26–27**, 36
minke whale 44
Moby Dick 40, *40*

N, O
narwhal 15, 27, 37, *37*
orca *see* killer whale

P
pantropical spotted dolphin 31
parasites 13, 15
pilot whale 10, 41, *41*, 46, *46*
pods 25, 29
pollution 32, 47
porpoising 31
prey 19, 20, 21, 28, 29

R
right whale 15
river dolphins **32–33**, *32*, *33*, 47

S
schools *see also* pods 6, *6*, 31, *31*
sei whale 10, 22
senses **16–17**
shepherd's beaked whale 11
skeleton 12, *12*, 13, *13*
smell, sense of 17
sounds 10, **24–25**, 29, 35, 36
spectacled porpoise 34, *34*, 35
sperm whale 9, 10, *10*, 19, *18–19*, 21, 40
spinner dolphin 30
spyhopping 17, 26
stranding 41, *41*
striped dolphin 31

T
taste, sense of 17
teeth 10, 20, 21, 34, 37, 39
toothed whales 10, 17, 20
touch, sense of 16
tracking 27, *27*
tucuxi dolphin 33

V, W, Y
vaquita 34, *34*
whale meat 43
whale stories 40
whale-watching 47
whalebone *see* baleen
whaling **42–43**, *42*, *43*, 46
Yangtze river dolphin 33, *33*